WITHDRAWN

Who's Got the
FACE?

Written by Doug Snelson
Illustrated by Renée Snelson

Petalous Publishing, LLC

Thank you to Renée, my daughter, for her wonderful illustrations and concepts; Ryan, my son, for his creative book design; Michele, my daughter-in-law, for her invaluable copyediting; and Diane, my wife and business partner, for her insight and unconditional support.

WHO'S GOT THE FACE?

Published by Petalous Publishing, LLC, PO Box 338, Montville, NJ 07045

Library of Congress Control Number: 200693182
ISBN-13: 978-0-9777811-0-2
ISBN-10: 0-9777811-0-0

Printed in the United States of America

First Edition

Book and cover design by Screenkind

To purchase this book visit petalous.com

For all the dogs we've known
who have "the face":

Angie
Annie
Bailey
Beauregard
Biscuit
Bobby
Brandy
Bristol
Brutus
Buffy
Butchie
Casey
Coco
Diesel
Duddley
Duke
Dusty
Finn
Fluffy
Frankie
Frosty
Ginsberg
Glory

Haley
Harley
Harvey
Honey
Indie
Jake
Jasper
Jazmin
Jessie
Jolie
Kraut
Lacey
Lola
Lucy
Maggie
Marcus
Max
Mayor Jack
Meetu
Misha
Missy
Moonshine
Mooshie

Muffin
Mugsy
Natasha
Nelson George
Oliver
Oscar
Panda
Papaya
Paws
Peanut
Pebbles
Pepi
Poco
Poochie
Rex
Rigley
Rocket
Rocky
Roxanne
Roxy
Rusty
Samantha
Sasha

Screech
Snowball
Solo
Sparky
Star
Summer
Sundance
Sunni
Sweeney
Swizzle
Tahoe
Tater
Teddy
Thor
Tippy
Trusty
Zeke
Zoey

and especially, Bruce, Facey, and Suede.

I have a dog. His name is Face.
He's got the smiles all over the place!

Face struts around with a playful grin.

I call to him as his day begins!

Who's got the face?
Who likes to chase?

Who runs the house
at such a fast pace?

Who's got the face?
Who's got the eyes?

Who digs holes for a hidden surprise?

Who's got the face?

Who's got the ears?

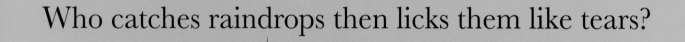

Who catches raindrops then licks them like tears?

Who's got the face?
Who's got the nose?

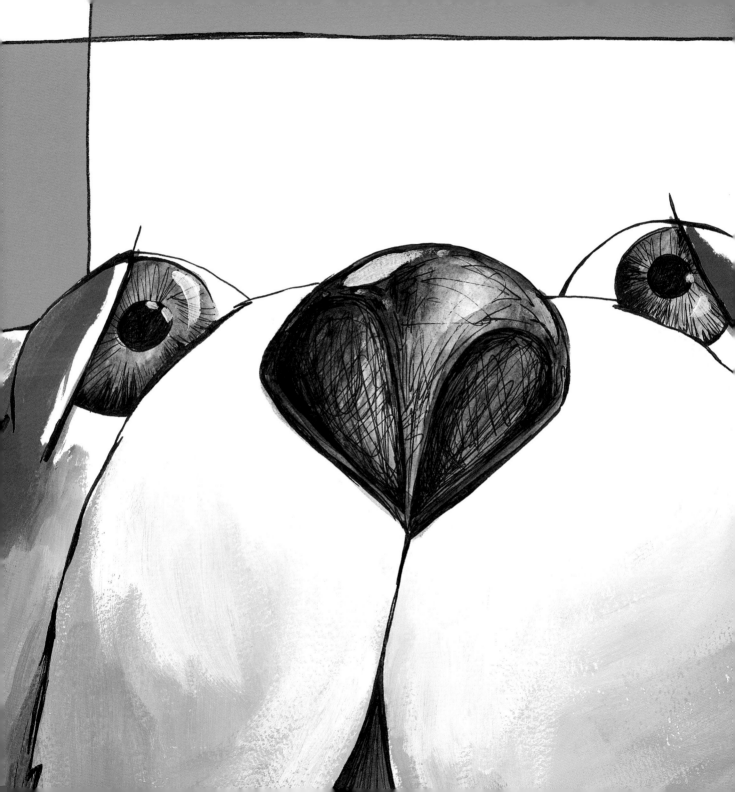

Who sniffs my socks in all the clean clothes?

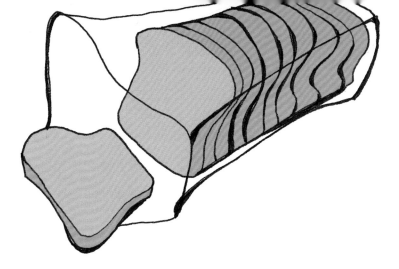

Who's got the face?
Who's got the belly?

Who eats my peanut butter and jelly?

Who's got the face?
Who's got the wag?

Who waves his tail like a furry flag?

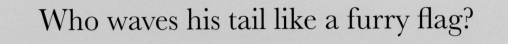

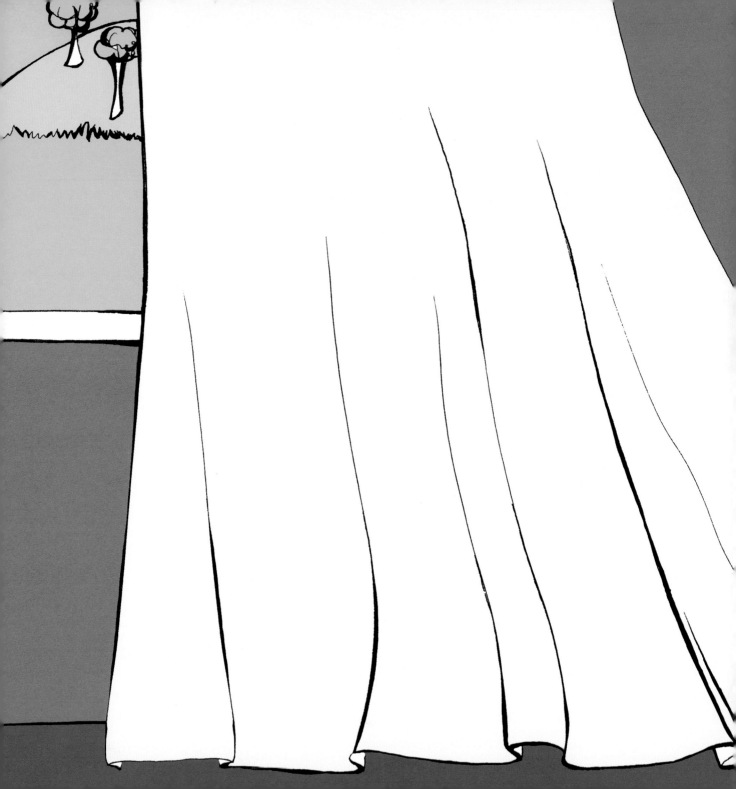

Who's got the face?
Who plays hide and seek?

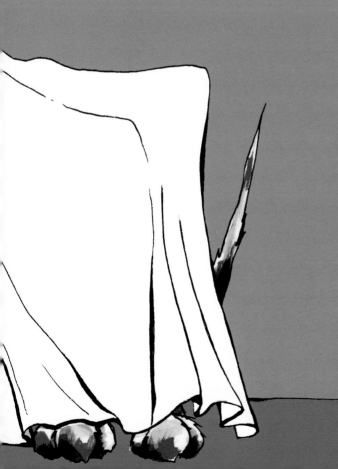

Who disappears then gives me a peek?

Who's got the face?
Who's got the paws?

Who shakes my hand for a dog bone applause?

Who's got the face?
Who's got the heart?

Who gives me love?
We're never apart.

Who closes his eyes? Who looks for his bed?

Who drops his tail with his paws near his head?

That's my dog, Face. You know he's the best.

Now it's time to sleep.
My friend needs a rest.